MEGA MASH-UP

Romans v Dinosaurs on Mars

Draw your own adventure!

Nikalas Catlow
Tim Wesson

nosy crow

Mega Mash-Up: Romans v Dinosaurs on Mars

Published in the UK in 2011 by Nosy Crow Ltd
Crow's Nest, 704 The Chandlery
50 Westminster Bridge Road
London, SE1 7QY, UK

Registered office: 85 Vincent Square, London, SW1P 2PF, UK

A CIP catalogue record for this book is available from the British Library

ISBN: 978 0 85763 001 8

Your hand

This book needs

YOU!

What if the ROMANS and DINOSAURS lived on **MARS?** What if a HUGE ASTEROID was about to crash into the planet and **exPLODE?** What would they all do? Would they invent something :SPECTACULAR: and then have some FUN AND GAMES? You'll have to finish the illustrations and find out...

Prepare to **LAUGH** while you doodle and SNIGGER while you read.

You'll need these...

DRAWING tools

These are the **3** tools that Nikalas and Tim have used to create the artwork in this book.

felt-tip pen or marker

pencil

wax crayon

PEN

crayon

Using different tools helps create great drawings

texture page

pen zigzags

crayon rubbing from lino floor

cross-hatching pencil

crayon rubbing from floor

pencil rubbing from wooden door

scribbly pencil

There are loads of ways you can add texture to your artwork. Here are a few examples

crayon rubbing from floor

pencil dashes

pen circles

DRAWING TIP! Turn to the back of the book for ideas on stuff you might want to draw in this adventure

INTRODUCING the ROMANS of ROMASAURIA!

★Augustus Astronomus★

★Grittus Cementus★

★ Maximus Victorious ★

★Ingenius Inventus★

★ Marcus Linus ★

INTRODUCING the Dinosaurs of Romasauria!

★ Eurekadon ★

★ Caesardon ★

★ Raptor Remedus ★

★ Tiberius Rex ★

★ Clawdius ★

Chapter 1
In the
Beginning

The **ROMANS** and **DINOSAURS** live together in a huge glass dome on Mars called **ROMASAURIA**. They are not exactly the best of friends.

Extend the hover road

Two dinosaurs, **CLAWDIUS** and **CAESARDON**, are discussing their Roman neighbours. "It's all roads, roads, roads with them," complains Clawdius.

"I know," grumbles Caesardon. "What's wrong with **SQUELCHING** through the primordial **SWAMP** like the rest of us?"

Not far away, Grittus Cementus is laying down paving for another new **HOVER ROAD.** "Hurry up! I want to get the lines painted before those **MUDDY GREAT DINOSAURS** come along!" shouts Marcus Linus.

Other road works here

Roman at work sign

Soon all is ready for a spectacular Rocket Chariot Race. Two chariots are zooming around while the crowd goes crazy! "**GO, TiBERiuS REX**!" roar the Dinosaurs. "**HaiL, MaXimuS ViCTORiouS**!" chant the Romans. "And what a splendid road!"

Maximus Victorious wins the race!

"Thanks for the trophy and stuff," says the triumphant Roman.

"HaiL! HaiL! HaiL!" chant the crowd.

Show a Dinosaur being thrown into the air

Show a sandal being thrown into the air

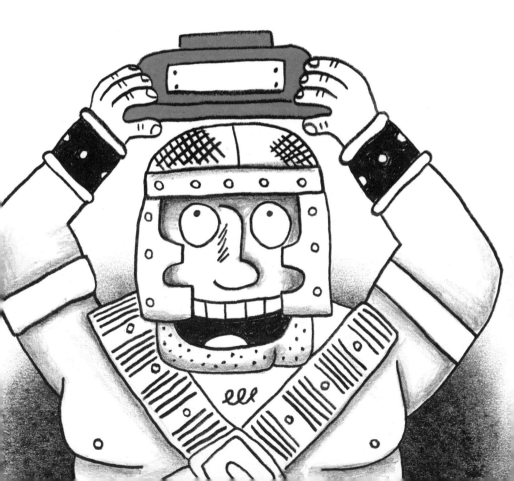

Give Maximus a giant trophy

A celebratory feast of **MOON-COW AND CHIPS** is served. The sound of munching can be heard all over Romasauria. Caesardon lets out a huge **BUUUUURRP**. "Manners!" splutters Grittus Cementus, spraying the table with chewed up moon-cow. How gross!

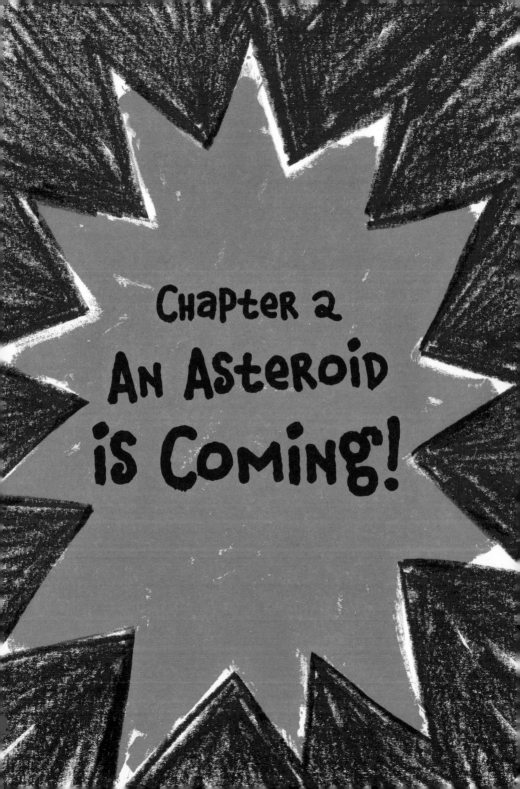

Chapter 2
An Asteroid is Coming!

What's in here?

Fill the cabinet with wacky potions

MASTER-MAGICIAN Raptor Remedus is in his lab creating a miraculous mix to cure all the ills in Romasauria.

Who's on the end of the tube?

ONE DROP of the potion gives **CARROTASAURUS X-RAY VISION.** "Shall I use my power for good or evil?" he ponders.

Evil thought in here

Two DROPS gives Tinyearus **SUPER HEARING**. "I can listen to everything that is going on in Romasauria!" he exclaims.

WOW... What kind
of things can he hear?

THREE DROPS cures wrinkles and boils.

However, there are side effects.

"Don't worry about those, er, I don't think they're permanent," stutters Raptor Remedus.

FOUR DROPS accidentally fall on a passing Minidon.
It is turned rock solid. "OOPS," says Raptor Remedus.
"Still, such a power could be useful one day!"

UH-OH! Some other Dinos have been turned solid!

A perfect opportunity to draw some still life!

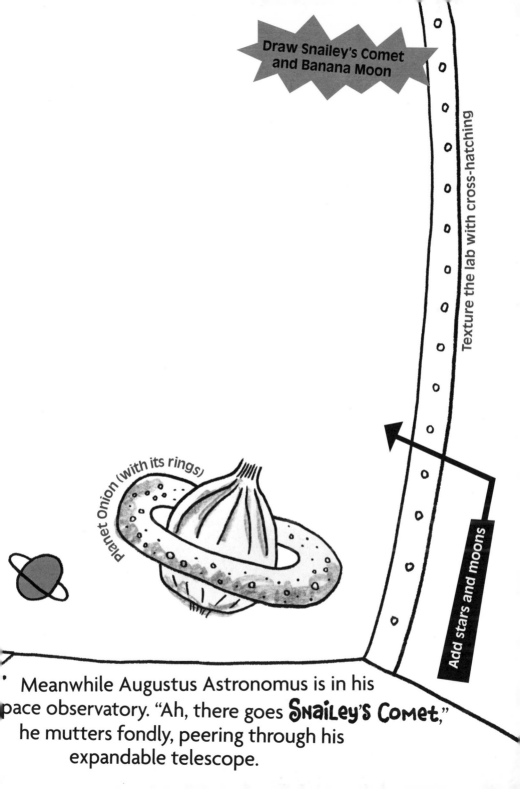

Draw Snailey's Comet and Banana Moon

Texture the lab with cross-hatching

Planet Onion (with its rings)

Add stars and moons

Meanwhile Augustus Astronomus is in his space observatory. "Ah, there goes **SNaiLey's Comet**," he mutters fondly, peering through his expandable telescope.

SUDDENLY Augustus spots something that nearly blows his sandals off! A massive asteroid is on a collision course with Romasauria. "**BLESS MY TOGA!** It will hit this afternoon!"

Use a crayon to fill in the sky

Add more planets and stars

Shade in the observatory

Add more craters and shading

Add aliens to the craters!

Augustus doesn't waste time. He races up the paved street to the top of Romasauria where the great **HORN OF PANDAEMONIUS** has stood idle for many years. He blows three long warning **toots** on the horn, which echo all around the dome.

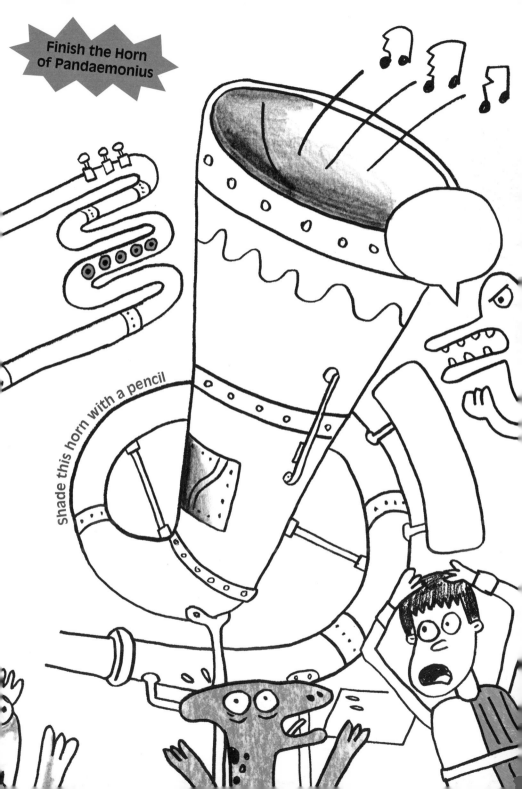

Who else is on the Town Hall steps?

This pillar needs a statue

The news about the
asteroid travels fast.
There is widespread **Panic** in Romasauria.
"Fear not!" cries Caesardon. "We will think of something.
Er ... any ideas?"

Chapter 3
The Roman way

Ingenius Inventus steps forward. "Stand aside, coming through!" he announces, dragging a large **WOODEN MACHINE.** "What in the name of Romasauria is that?" puzzle the crowd.

Who's sneaked into the sling?

"It's a catapult," explains Ingenius.
"A really **Heavy Dinosaur** climbs into the sling,
then we pull the lever, the Dinosaur plummets
to the ground and the machine flings
deadly sandals at the asteroid
and breaks it into a
1000 Pieces!"
"**Hurrah!**"
cheer the Romans.

There's no need for that!

Put a heavy
Dinosaur
in the sling

"What did you say about deadly sandals?" asks Caesardor

"The deadly sandals are flung at the asteroid and — " But Ingenius's words are drowned out by the Dinosaurs' **HONKING** laughter. "**Ha ha ha ha ha ha!** That's the funniest thing we've ever heard!"

Help Ingenius explain his idea

DEADLY SANDAL

What are the cheeky Dinosaurs saying?

Draw your own laughing Dinosaur

The Romans are cross. All eyes turn to Eurekadon, who **WHIPS** the cloth away from an invention of his own... "Ta-da! Friends, Romans, countrymen – I give you the **TORPOODO**! It is Dinosaur dung, squished and baked in the Mars' sun. It will Save the Day!"

Show the huge asteroid coming!

Texture the rock

"We will form a mighty tower of Dinosaurs, then the smallest one will lob TorPOOdoes at the asteroid, breaking it into 1000 pieces!"

"That's the **silliest** thing I've ever heard!" scoffs Inventus.
"The TorPOOdo would be too squidgy."
"Right, toga-boy, that's it..." snarls Eurekadon.
"Oh yes, lizard-face, **you and whose centurions**?"
A fight kicks off. "Eat my deadly sandal!" says Ingenius.
"TorPOOdoes away!" cries Eurekadon.

"Oh, this won't do, only **MAGIC** can save us now," wails Caesardon. Tinysaurus pushes his way through the crowd. "Did you say **MAGIC**?" he splutters. "Raptor Remedus's **MAGIC** potion might just do the trick!"

What's behind Caesardon's back?

"By Georgasaurus, that's it!" shouts Clawdius.

"**Fetch the Potion, fast!**" Tinysaurus pegs it across Romasauria as fast as his titchy legs will carry him...

Chapter 4
The Martian
Magician

QUEUE

What's in the window?

Texture rub the rest of the lab with cardboard

Tinysaurus explains the **WHOLE** situation to Raptor Remedus at **TOP SPEED**. "Four drops of the magic potion on each TorPOOdo should be enough," he says. "But be quick, its effects do not last long." He points at a passing Minidon.
"Long enough," says the Minidon, crossly.

Add the potion bottle

SPARE HEADS AND STUFF

Ooh... Stick a head in it

What else lurks on the shelves?

Texture rub the rest of the stone shelving

Finish the crowd

Draw the opened magic potion bottle

BACK AT THE TOWN HALL...

"I've got it, I've got it!" pants Tinysaurus.
"Four drops will make the TorPOOdoes as hard as, er,
REALLY HARD STUFF!" "Hurrah!" cheers Ingenius.
"We'll launch the mega-hard TorPOOdoes
from my catapult!"

Time has nearly run out, the asteroid **IS COMING**! Will magic Dinosaur poo flung by a giant catapult really save them all from **DOOM**?

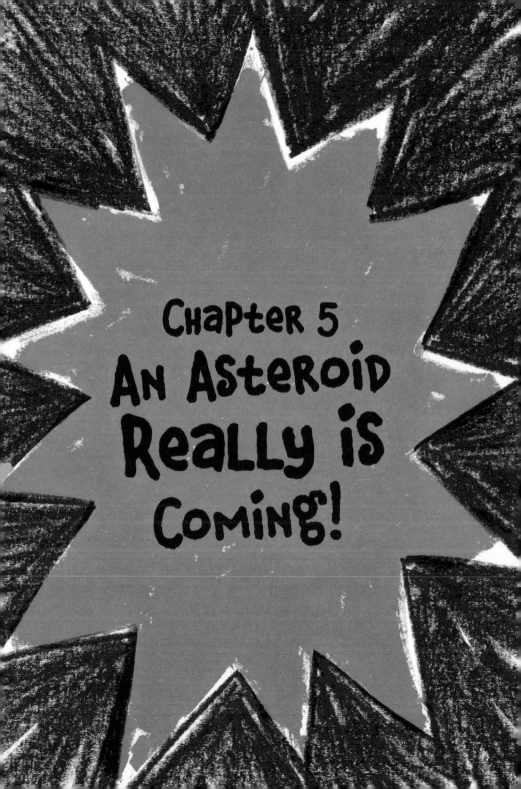

Chapter 5
An Asteroid
Really is
Coming!

The Dinosaurs form a queue which **SNakeS** into the woods. Will they have enough loo roll to go round? The fresh poo is then squished into TorPOOdo-shapes and left out to bake in the Mars' sun.

"Add the potion!" shouts Eurekadon, and the Romasaurians start dropping it on to the pongy poo bricks. "**HURRaH!**" they cheer, holding their noses.

Create a few little Dinosaurs desperate for the loo. Ha ha!

He needs a toilet roll fast!

Suddenly Augustus Astronomus shouts, "It's coming!"
Lardosaurus heaves himself into the sling,
("**OOF!**"), the rope is cut **(TWANG!)** and the
TorPOOdoes are flung into outer space **(KERFLUNK!)**.

Draw a pile
of TorPOOdoes

Romasauria hangs in **SUSPENSE** as they watch
the TorPOOdoes disappear into the night sky. "If this
doesn't work we'll be **FLATTENED**!" whines the crowd.
They wait, and wait ... then...

Who else is wearing space helmets?

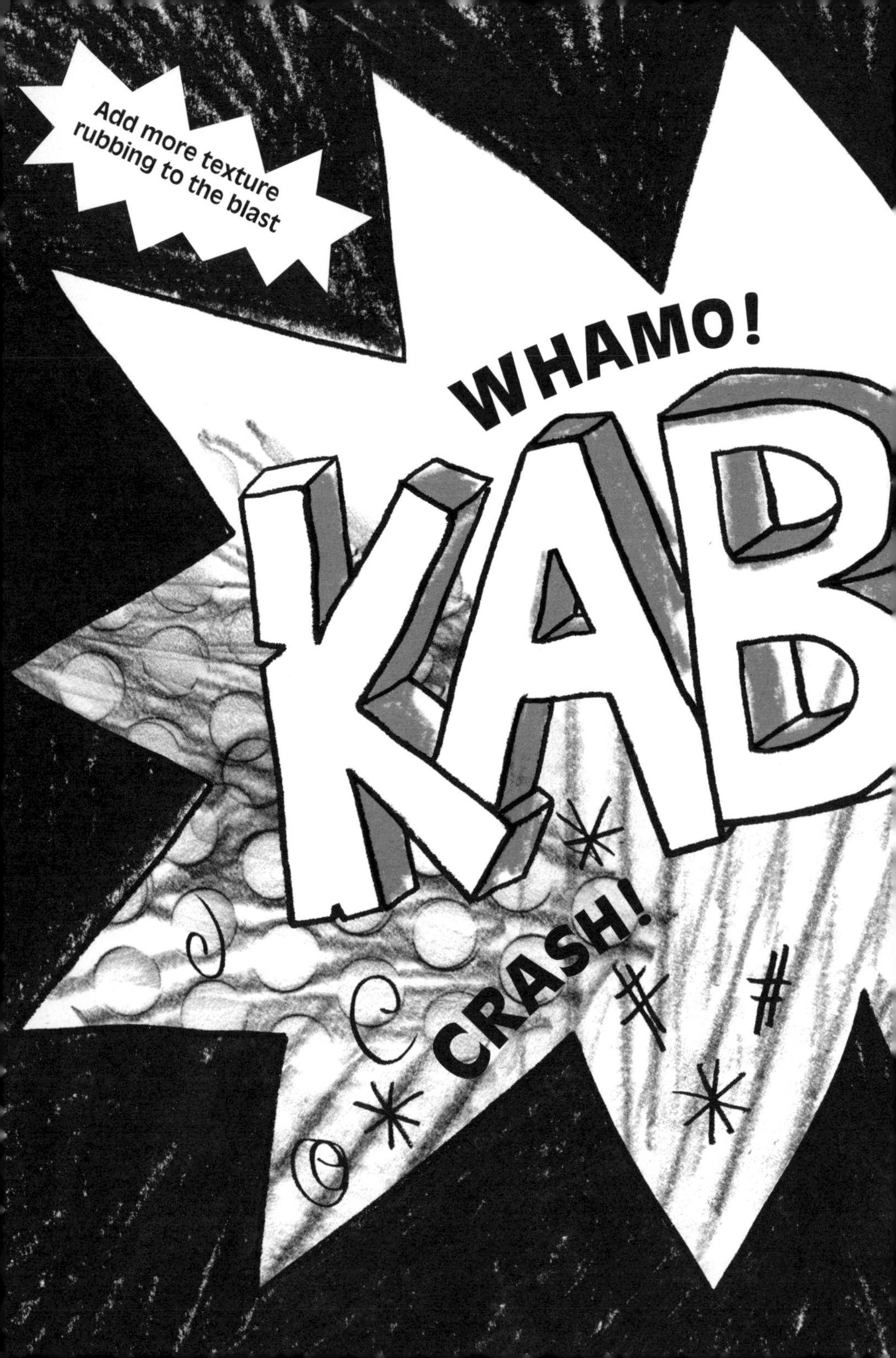
Add more texture rubbing to the blast
WHAMO!
KAB
CRASH!

Add a smaller KABLAM and mini KABOOMS
kaboom
OOM
Boom
What other sounds do explosions make?

A huge explosion rips through the sky, then all is quiet again. Until large lumps of **MeLteD** asteroid and poo start to fall to Mars.

Add a few more lumps of TorPOOdo and asteroid

IT'S WORKED!

"HURRAH!" the Romasaurians cheer.
"WE'RE SAVED! WE'RE SAVED!
WE'RE SAVED!"

What else is being thrown in the air to celebrate?

Now that Romasauria has been saved, the Romans and Dinosaurs decide to celebrate. **"Let's have some fun and games!"** shout Ingenius and Eurekadon.

dd more buildings in the background

TICKETS

This stall needs a sign. What tasty treats are being sold?

Wow! What does an angry POOgoid look like?

The first game is called "Herd the POOgoid!"
Who is brave enough to face the
STINKIEST CREATURE on Mars?
"POOP POOP POOP!" goes the POOgoid.
The crowd go wild!

Add small rocks and shading to texture the ground

The crowd chant **"CLiNG ON!"** as the next event gets under way. Who will be the first to drop into a stinky swamp dung pit?

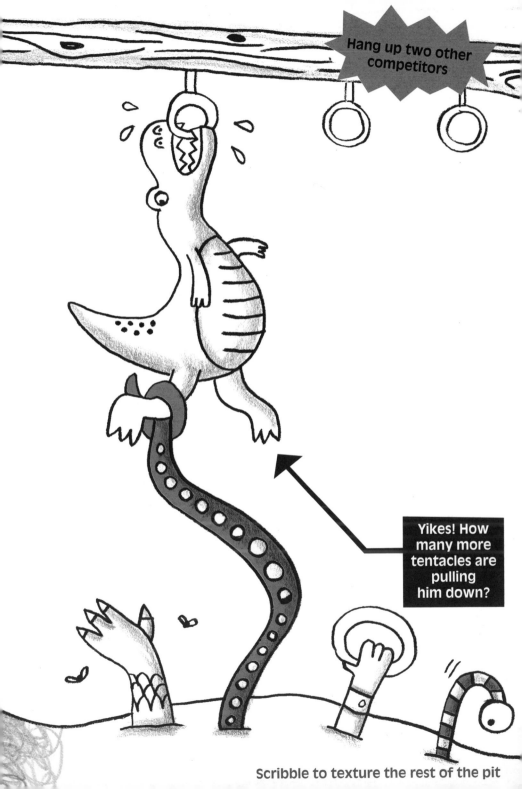

Finally, they decide to have a giant **tug-of-war.**
"**Heave!**" grunt the Dinosaurs.

"Long live Romasauria!" cries the crowd, and the closing ceremony comes to an end with a brilliant TorPOOdo **SaLute.** "Long live Romasauria!" "Can I get out of this sling now?" asks Lardosaurus, wearily.

Who's the winner? You decide

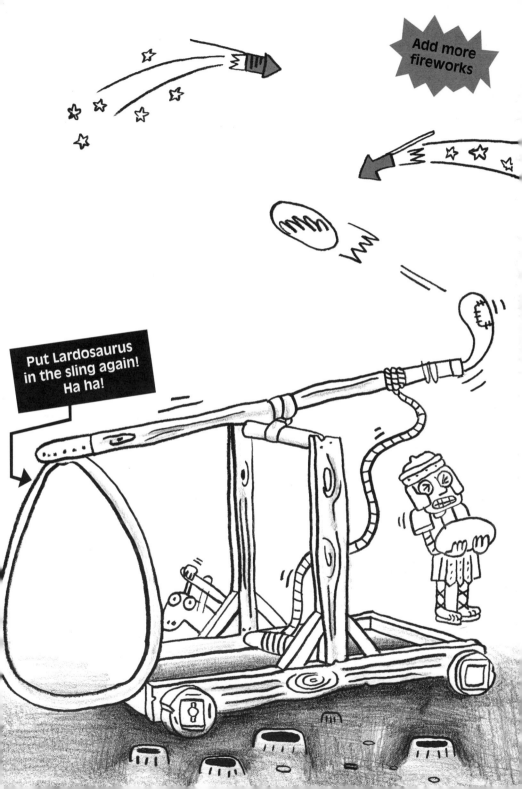

They all decide to have a feast to celebrate.
The table is groaning with Roman goodies and
Dinosaur treats. "Have a **ROaSt JeLLy
MaRTian GerbiL**," offers Grittus Cementus.

Who else is having a food fight?

Add a nice big bowl of lizard entrails!

"Don't mind if I do," accepts Clawdius.

"And please, do try some regurgitated **LizaRD eNTRaiLS.**" Grittus Cementus goes green and has to leave the table.

What an eventful time it's been in Romasauria!
They created a **magic potion**, invented a **TorpOOdo**
and destroyed an asteroid using a **giant catapult!**
But in the end it was all just **fun and games!**

Picture Glossary

If you get stuck or need ideas, then use these pages for reference.

Doughnut Globe

PLANETS AND COSMIC STUFF

Banana Moon

Rocky Moon

Planet Hairy

Snailey's Comet

ROMAN COSTUME

Formal

Casual

A ROMAN AND A DINOSAUR ARGUING

CHARACTER EXPRESSIONS

Angry Roman   Curious Roman

Curious Dinosaur

Angry Dinosaur

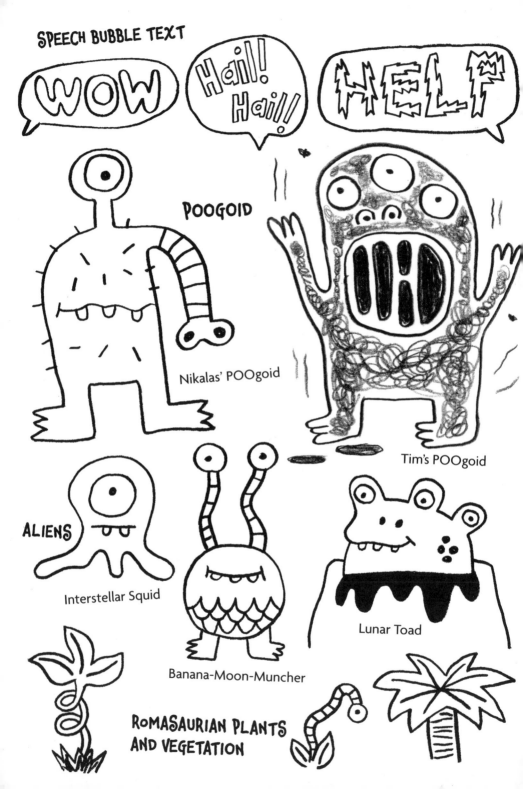